Saffron
Ice Cream

Rashin
Kheiriyeh

ARTHUR A. LEVINE BOOKS

AN IMPRINT OF SCHOLASTIC INC.

To my parents, who created a happy childhood for me.

LIBRARY OF CONGRESS CATALOGING-IN-PUBLICATION DATA

Names: Kheiriyeh, Rashin, author, illustrator. | Title: Saffron ice cream / by Rashin Kheiriyeh. Description: First edition. | New York, NY : Arthur A. Levine Books, an imprint of Scholastic Inc., 2018. | Summary: Rashin is an Iranian immigrant girl living in New York, excited by her first trip to Coney Island, and fascinated by the differences in the beach customs between her native Iran and her new home—but she misses the saffron flavored ice cream that she used to eat. | Identifiers: LCCN 2017041205 | ISBN 9781338150520 (hardcover : alk. paper) | Subjects: LCSH: Immigrant children—New York (State)—New York—Juvenile fiction. | Iranians—United States—Juvenile fiction. | Muslims—Social life and customs—Juvenile fiction. | Coney Island (New York, N.Y.)—Juvenile fiction. | United States—Social life and customs—Juvenile fiction. | CYAC: Immigrants—Fiction. | Iranian Americans—Fiction. | Muslims—Fiction. | Coney Island (New York, N.Y.)—Fiction. | United States—Social life and customs—Fiction. | Classification: LCC PZ7.1.K533 Saf 2018 | DDC [E]—dc23 LC record available at https://lccn.loc.gov/2017041205

ISBN 978-1-338-15052-0

10 9 8 7 6 5 4   19 20 21 22 23

Printed in China 38 | First edition, June 2018

The text type was set in Century Gothic Bold and Janda Curlygirl Chun.
The display type was set in KG Kiss Me Slowly Regular.
The artwork was created using oil and acrylic on handmade textured paper.
Book design by Marijka Kostiw

My name is Rashin.

And this is my first trip to the beach!

Oh, not just to ANY beach —

I mean to an American beach. In Brooklyn.

That's where I live now.

When

I lived in Iran, we used to drive to the
Caspian Sea to swim. Very early in the morning,
my mom would mix together wheat, turkey,
sugar, and cinnamon to make halim for breakfast.

Then we
would pack into my dad's old car and
head toward a very green and beautiful
part of Iran called Shomal. We'd drive for about
five hours, listening to Persian music on the radio
and stopping to eat a picnic lunch in the
forest along the way. Sometimes I took along
my friend, Azadeh, and we'd share a kebab.

The beach in Brooklyn is called

Coney Island.

We're getting there by subway train,

which is filled with all sorts of people — and ALSO has music.

But no Azadeh.

In Iran,

the Caspian Sea looked endless, blue, and beautiful.

How will the sea look in Brooklyn?

In some

parts of the Caspian beach, there are beach rules, so I knew what was

allowed. In that part of the beach, big, long curtains divided the sea

into two sections — one side for men to swim in and the other side for women.

My dad and my brother would go

to the male section.

Ice Cream

بستنی زعفرانی

Saffron

. . . which is

the exciting part of the beach. It is like a big party!

Women take off their covers and get a tan.

Everyone was female there:

me, Azadeh, our moms — even the

ice cream seller.

One day,

I was swimming along with Azadeh when, suddenly,

I noticed some little holes in the curtain. I could swear

I saw eyes blinking behind them! Suddenly Azadeh saw them

too and screamed, "Boys, boys, boys!"

Three little boys who had climbed onto each other's shoulders fell down into the water.

SPLASH!

Then the

other women joined in, shouting and jumping

out of the water and covering themselves

with towels, newspapers, and umbrellas.

The Islamic

beach guards ran to fix the holes in the curtain.

It was chaos! But it was fun.

Will it be fun in Brooklyn too?

When we get off the Q train at Ocean Parkway,

it's a fun chaos too, though I don't know anybody.

Families of all colors stream from the redbrick apartment buildings.

The sidewalk vibrates with music, and kids chase each other.

A block from the beach, my mother points to a truck
with a window in it, and a small line of kids
jumping up and down. "Look, Rashin," says my mother.
"An ice cream seller. Just like back home."

Well, not just like,

I think. But I wait on that line, hoping, hoping they will have the delicious saffron flavor Azadeh and I used to love so much.

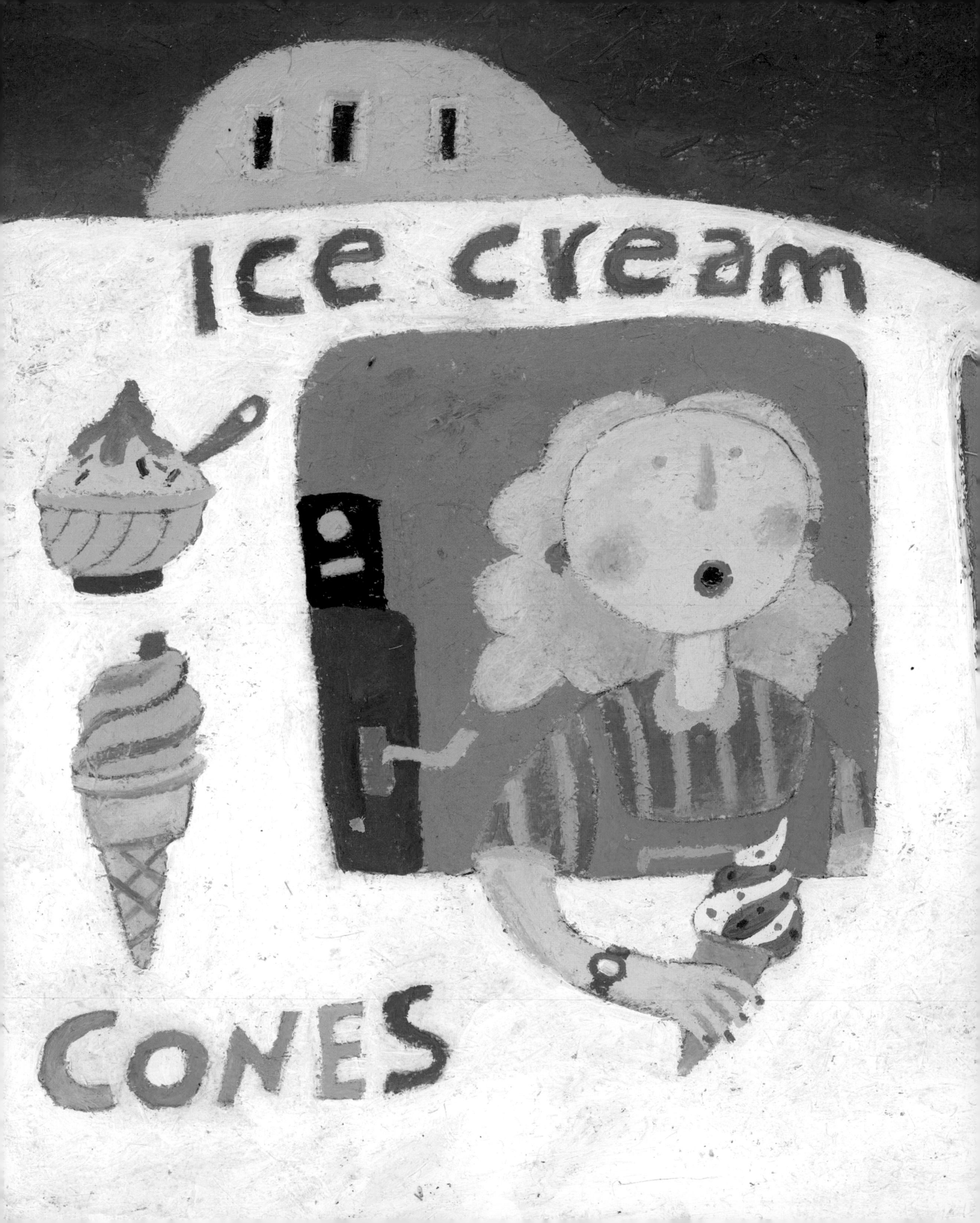
ice cream
CONES

"Sorry, sweetheart," says the lady in the truck window.

"No saffron. Would you like something else?"

I can't help it. I start to cry. I miss the Caspian Sea.

I miss Azadeh. I miss everything.

"Hey, kid. Try chocolate crunch! That's MY favorite,"

says a sweet-faced girl with brown skin and a bright orange shirt.

She is smiling, so I smile too and feel a little better.

Turns out

chocolate crunch is a pretty good

flavor too. I can't wait to write and tell

Azadeh all about it.

But first we get to the beach, and my family spreads out
blankets all together — men and women! The beach is so wide
and covered with umbrellas and blankets and people.

But there, not so far, is the girl I met at the ice cream truck,
and she waves at me.

Then I walk up to the girl and practice what I've learned.

"Hi," I say. "My name is Rashin. What is yours?"

"Hi! I'm Aijah. Want to swim?"

I look toward my mother and she nods.

"First, I have question," I say.

I hope I'm saying it right.

"What are the rules

for the beach?"

"Good question!"

she says. "My dad says I have to stay where he and the lifeguard can see us. And not to go too far out.

"Another important rule is . . .

"... to have fun, fun, fun."

I'm sure there are other beach rules to learn.

But that seems like a good place to start!